anythink

Come Back, Moon

by David Kherdian
Illustrated by Nonny Hogrogian

Beach Lane Books
New York   London   Toronto   Sydney   New Delhi

BEACH LANE BOOKS

An imprint of Simon & Schuster Children's Publishing Division

1230 Avenue of the Americas, New York, New York 10020

Copyright © 2013 by Nonny Hogrogian and David Kherdian

All rights reserved, including the right of reproduction in whole or in part in any form.

BEACH LANE BOOKS is a trademark of Simon & Schuster, Inc.

For information about special discounts for bulk purchases, please contact Simon & Schuster Special Sales at

1-866-506-1949 or business@simonandschuster.com.

The Simon & Schuster Speakers Bureau can bring authors to your live event. For more information or to book an event,

contact the Simon & Schuster Speakers Bureau at 1-866-248-3049 or visit our website at www.simonspeakers.com.

Design by Sonia Chaghatzbanian

The text for this book is set in Bembo.

The illustrations for this book are rendered in watercolor and pencil.

Manufactured in China

0713 SCP

First Edition

2 4 6 8 10 9 7 5 3 1

Library of Congress Cataloging-in-Publication Data

Kherdian, David.

Come back, moon / by David Kherdian ; illustrated by Nonny Hogrogian. — 1st ed.

p. cm.

Summary: A sleepless bear hides the moon, much to the displeasure of his forest animal friends

who miss dancing under its light.

ISBN 978-1-4424-5887-1

ISBN 978-1-4424-5888-8 (eBook)

[1. Moon—Fiction. 2. Bears—Fiction. 3. Forest animals—Fiction.]

I. Hogrogian, Nonny, illustrator. II. Title.

PZ7.K527Co 2013

[E]—dc23 2012037038

Bear couldn't sleep and blamed the light of the moon.

So Bear stole the moon.

No one knew where the moon had gone.

"It's gone," said Fox.

"Where did it go?" asked Skunk.

"I miss the moon," said Opossum.

"Maybe someone stole it," Raccoon said.

"Don't you know?" Crow asked Fox. "You're the clever one. Where did it go?"

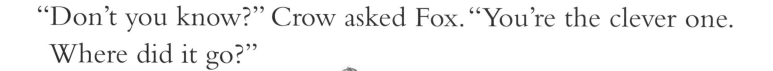

"I may be clever," Fox said, "but Owl is wise. Let's ask Owl."

"Let's ask Owl," said Opossum.

"Let's ask Owl," said Skunk.

"Let's ask Owl," said Raccoon.

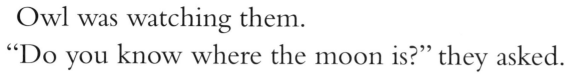

Owl was watching them.
"Do you know where the moon is?" they asked.

"I saw Bear take the moon," Owl said.

"Bear?" cried the other animals.
"Bear," said Owl. "Bear stole the moon."

"Let's go," Fox said. "Let's go get the moon back from Bear."

"Let's go!" they all said.

And off they went to Bear's camp.

"Tell Bear a story," Fox said to Crow,
"and put him to sleep. I will look for the moon."

So Crow told a story, and soon Bear dozed off.
Fox saw the moon glowing inside Bear's pillow.

Quickly, Fox and Crow grabbed the pillow bag and set the moon free.

And all the animals cheered and danced under the light of the moon.

All except Bear, who was happily sound asleep.